SANTA IN THE CITY

written by Tiffany D. Jackson   illustrated by Reggie Brown

Dial Books for Young Readers

Every year, Deja counted down the days, hours, minutes, seconds, until Christmas.

But some kids at school didn't believe in Santa like she did.

"If there's a Santa, how does he get into your apartment when there's no chimney?" DeShawn asked. "That sleigh can't fit nowhere and reindeer can't fly!"

"And no one can live up at the North Pole," Carmen said. "Face it, Deja, there is no Santa! Even if there was, he'd never visit us in the city."

That night, Mommy found Deja
in her room crying.

"What's wrong, Deja?"

"Mommy, tell me the truth. Is there
really a Santa Claus?"

"Of course there is, baby girl!"

"But how does Santa get inside our house if we don't have a chimney?"

Mommy smiled. "Deja, magic always finds a way! Come, let me show you."

③

④

WELCO

She took Deja down to the first floor, where Mr. Clark was painting the front door. She pointed to the big keychain hanging off his tool belt.

"Santa's got a special keychain like our super, Mr. Clark. His key is magic and opens up all the apartments in the entire world."

"Oh," Deja said. Makes sense.

"Okay, but where does he park his sleigh? There's no free parking spots on our block at night and ain't none of them big enough for nine reindeers!"

Mommy laughed. "He parks on the roof just like he does at everyone else's house."

She took Deja by the hand and led her up on the top floor, pointing to the roof door.

"See?" Mommy said, "Santa comes in through there." She showed Deja where Santa parked his sleigh and the old pigeon feeder Mr. Clark used to give the reindeer a snack.

"Oh," Deja said. Makes sense.

Satisfied, Deja took the stairs back down to her apartment.

SLEIGH PARKING

As Mommy tucked her into bed and read her favorite Christmas book,
Deja smiled. DeShawn and Carmen were wrong; Santa did come to their city.

But the next morning, as Deja left for a day of Christmas shopping with Mommy, she couldn't help noticing how different her neighborhood looked from ones in her book. The buildings on her block didn't seem ready for Christmas.

She tugged on Mommy's coat. "If we can't decorate our building, how will Santa find us?"

"The mayor puts up extra special lights all around the neighborhood," Mommy said. "And we always put lights in our windows, so Santa won't miss us."

"Oh," Deja said. Makes sense.

ORTIZ BODEGA

DELI & GROCERY 102682

Lotto
Here

Eggs
Huevos

Ice Cream
Paletas
Snacks
Patata frita

But as soon as they walked into the corner bodega, another question popped into Deja's head.

And then another.

And another!

She almost didn't hear Mr. Ortiz say her breakfast sandwich was ready.

"Hey Lil' Mami, what's on your mind?" Mr. Ortiz asked.

"Mr. Ortiz, can reindeer really fly?"

"Si mami! They're just like chickens. They can fly short distances, hopping from block to block till they reach our block."

$1.75

Chips
$1.00

Fruta Fresca

GUM   GUM

WATER

Chips

DEMI

"Oh," Deja said. Makes sense.

KINGS PLAZA

Santaland

But even later that afternoon, as Deja and Mommy finished shopping, her head was so full of questions, she thought she might burst! She pointed to Santaland and asked, "Okay, how can Santa be at Kings Plaza, at Macy's, and up at the North Pole making all our presents at the same time?"

"Well, those men are Special Elves representing Santa. They listen to the wishes of all the little kids around the world, then report back to the big boss, Ol' St. Nick."

"Oh," Deja said. Makes sense.

ELF RUN

The next day was Christmas Eve, and Deja's entire family gathered at her auntie's house, where they had a big feast.

She played games with her cousins and danced with her uncles like she did every year, but it was hard to enjoy herself like she used to. She still had so many questions about Santa. And luckily, there were lots of people around to ask.

"Uncle Ronnie, how can Santa live up at the North Pole?
It's really cold up there!" Deja asked.

"Well, Santa works in tunnels underground, like
the subway, where it's much warmer.
Plus, he drinks plenty of hot cocoa."

"Oh," Deja said. Makes sense.

"What about when we visit Grandma and Pop-Pop in Jamaica? We're in a whole other country! How does he find us there?"

"Oh, that's easy," her auntie Kacy said. "Your mommy sends him a postcard to tell him where we'll all be."

SANTA

North Pole

"Oh," Deja said.
Makes sense.

Back at home, Deja left milk and cookies for Santa, but her head still swirled with questions.

Like, where do other kids put their stockings if they don't have a fireplace?

Or how does Santa make it to all their cities in one night? Or has he ever delivered presents to the wrong house like the mailman sometimes does?

"Doesn't Santa's tummy hurt after eating all the cookies everyone leaves him?" she asked Mommy.

"Santa doesn't eat all the cookies," Mommy said. "He eats some but has a magic sack he puts the rest in so he can share with the elves when he gets back to the North Pole. I've even packed them up for him."

"You mean, you've met Santa!"

"Yep. He asks grown-ups to help since he has lots of stops to make in one night."

"Oh," she said. That gave Deja an idea.

After Mommy tucked her into bed, Deja only pretended to go to sleep. Because there was only one person who could answer all her questions—Santa himself.

She waited until her mommy was asleep before sneaking out into the living room. But she just . . . couldn't . . . stay . . . awake.

She didn't hear Santa park his sleigh on the roof . . .

. . . or see him come down the steps.

. . . or use his magic key to open the door.

. . . or leave out the toys she asked the Special Elves for.

But when she woke up, she found something better than any toy. A special message from Santa, just for her, letting her know once and for all magic really does find a way.

Santa was real. And he had no problem coming to her city.

To Wynn and Nayara. With magic, you will always find a way.—T.J.

This book is dedicated to two angels that brought Christmas's joy alive
for us—our grandmothers Callie Donier Brown and Hilda Dillon Psellos.
May their memories be eternal, along with the magic of Christmas.—R.B.

Dial Books for Young Readers
An imprint of Penguin Random House LLC, New York

First published in the United States of America by Dial Books for Young Readers,
an imprint of Penguin Random House LLC, 2021

Text copyright © 2021 by Tiffany D. Jackson
Illustrations copyright © 2021 by Reggie Brown

Visit us online at penguinrandomhouse.com

Library of Congress Cataloging-in-Publication Data is available.

Manufactured in China
ISBN 9780593110256

10 9 8 7 6 5 4 3 2 1

HH

Design by Cerise Steel
Text set in KG Be Still And Know

The illustrations were created digitally using photoshop, and a pinch of Christmas magic.